# LET'S LOOK AT
# Colours

Nicola Tuxworth

LORENZ BOOKS

LONDON • NEW YORK • SYDNEY • BATH

# Red

Look at these red things.

a bottle of red ketchup

a juicy red tomato

a red hat

a red raincoat

a pair of warm red gloves

Have you got any red clothes?

two red parrots

a field of red poppies

three red
strawberries

a pretty
red rose

a shiny red pepper

# Blue

Look at these blue things.

a blue plaster

a blue glass bottle

blue eyes

blue clothes

What colour are your eyes?

a beautiful
blue sky

the deep blue sea

a blue fish
in the sea

a bunch of blue
flowers

a blue butterfly
on a leaf

# Yellow

Look at these yellow things.

three bright yellow flowers

a sour yellow lemon

a yellow T-shirt

yellow flowers

Are there any yellow flowers in your garden?

a tasty yellow banana

two yellow canaries

some yellow butter on a plate

a yellow chick and its eggshell

# Green

Look at these green things.

a bunch of green grapes

the insides of kiwi fruits

green apples

a green T-shirt

Are apples always green?

a spiny green iguana

three
green beans

a dark
green
leaf

a green frog in water

# Orange

Look at these orange things.

a crunchy orange carrot

a juicy orange orange

an orange iced lolly

an orange T-shirt

Do you like iced lollies?

a knobbly
orange starfish

an orange fish
in a bowl

an orange
pumpkin

# Pink

Look at these pink things.

a scented pink carnation

a pair of pink ballet shoes

a pink tutu

Do you like dancing?

a pretty pink lipstick

two pink piglets

four pale pink flamingoes

five pink fingernails

# Brown

Look at these brown things.

upside-down brown mushrooms

brown clothes

a big brown egg

a spiky brown pine cone

brown leaves

When do leaves turn brown?

a soft brown feather

some hard brown nuts

delicious brown chocolates

a brown bread roll

# Black

Look at these
black things.

a cat with
soft black fur

black
hair

some salty
black olives

a black
jumper

Is your hair black?

some sweet
black liquorice

a black chalkboard

a black
bow tie

a pair of
shiny black
shoes

# White

Look at these
white things.

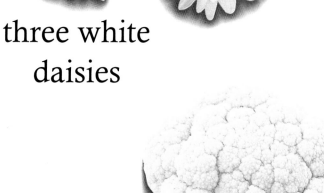

three white
daisies

white
teeth

a white shirt

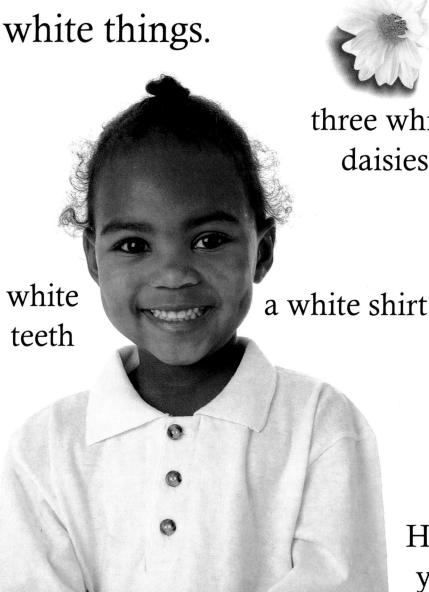

a white
cauliflower

How can you keep
your teeth white?

a bowl of
white rice

four sticks of
white chalk

a white water lily that
has just opened

a lacy
white
pillow

How many blue things
can you see?

What is the red
thing called?

Is the bow tie
green?

What is your
favourite colour?